D0118650

I SEE SOMETHING YOU DON'T SEE

I SEE SOMETHING YOU DON'T SEE

A Riddle-me Picture Book

ROBIN MICHAL KOONTZ

COBBLEHILL/Dutton · New York

This book is for all our kinfolk

in Alabama, past and present.

Library of Congress Cataloging-in-Publication Data
Koontz, Robin Michal.
I see something you don't see / Robin Michal Koontz.
p.   cm.
Summary: Two children enjoying a summer day at
Grandma's entertain each other with rhyming riddles.
ISBN 0-525-65077-6
1. Riddles, Juvenile.   [1. Riddles.]   I. Title.
PN6371.5.K66   1992   818'5402—dc20   91-8025   CIP   AC

Published in the United States by
Cobblehill Books,
an affiliate of Dutton Children's Books,
a division of Penguin USA Inc.,
375 Hudson Street, New York, NY 10014
Typography and jacket design by Kathleen Westray
Printed in Hong Kong
First Edition
10 9 8 7 6 5 4 3 2 1

Riddle-me
riddle-me-ree,
I see something
you don't see.
Read each riddle
and if you dare,
look at the picture
the answer is there!

Riddle-me
riddle-me-ree,
I see something
you don't see.
I run all day
and never walk.
I tell you something
but I don't talk.

(7)

Riddle-me
riddle-me-ree,
I see something
you don't see.
A house with no windows
nor doors to behold.
Crack me open,
inside, I'm gold.

(9)

Riddle-me
riddle-me-ree,
I see something
you don't see.
When you look at my face
it's easy to see,
you're looking at you
when you're looking at me.

(11)

Riddle-me
riddle-me-ree,
I see something
you don't see.
Round like a plate,
flat as a chip,
holes like eyes,
but can't see a bit.

(13)

Riddle-me
riddle-me-ree,
I see something
you don't see.
Soft as a petal
that falls from a tree,
the more I dry,
the wetter I'll be.

(15)

Riddle-me
riddle-me-ree,
I see something
you don't see.
I'm inside and outside,
I'm short or I'm tall.
You look at me
to see through a wall.

(17)

Riddle-me
riddle-me-ree,
I see something
you don't see.
Fluffy and light,
I live in the sky,
my shape ever-changing
as I go by.

(19)

Riddle-me
riddle-me-ree,
I see something
you don't see.
The warmer it gets,
the more I wear.
But when it's cold,
I am quite bare.

(21)

Riddle-me
riddle-me-ree,
I see something
you don't see.
In sand and in mud,
I'm easy to find.
You're always in front,
I'm always behind.

(23)

Riddle-me
riddle-me-ree,
I see something
you don't see.
I don't have feet
to skip or hop,
yet I can run
and never stop.

Riddle-me
riddle-me-ree,
I see something
you don't see.
In bright sunshine,
I'm always here.
But turn off the lights
and I disappear.

Riddle-me
riddle-me-ree,
I see something
you don't see.
I'm like a garden
of blossoms bright
that only blooms
in dark of night.

(29)

Riddle-me
riddle-me-ree,
I see something
you don't see.
I have legs
but never run.
Tuck yourself in,
and wait for the sun.

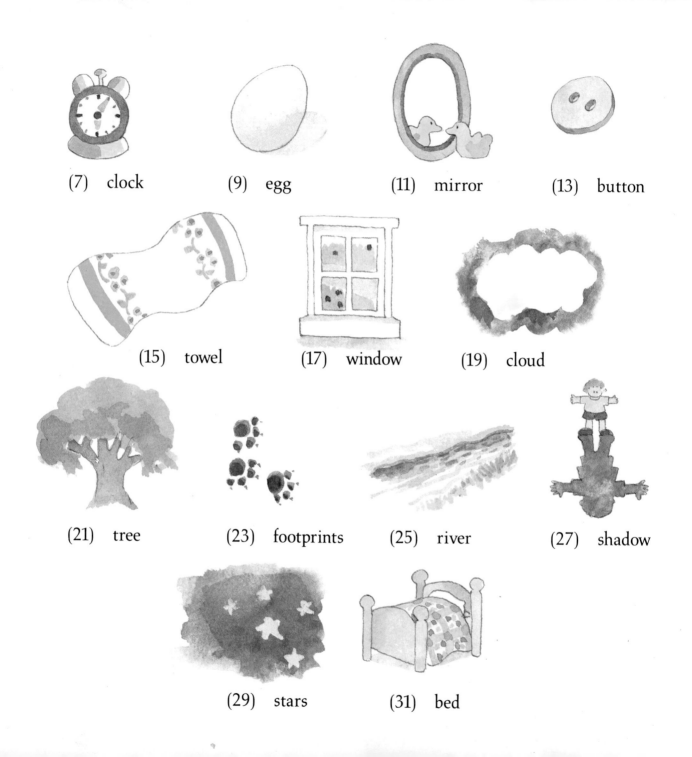

(7) clock

(9) egg

(11) mirror

(13) button

(15) towel

(17) window

(19) cloud

(21) tree

(23) footprints

(25) river

(27) shadow

(29) stars

(31) bed